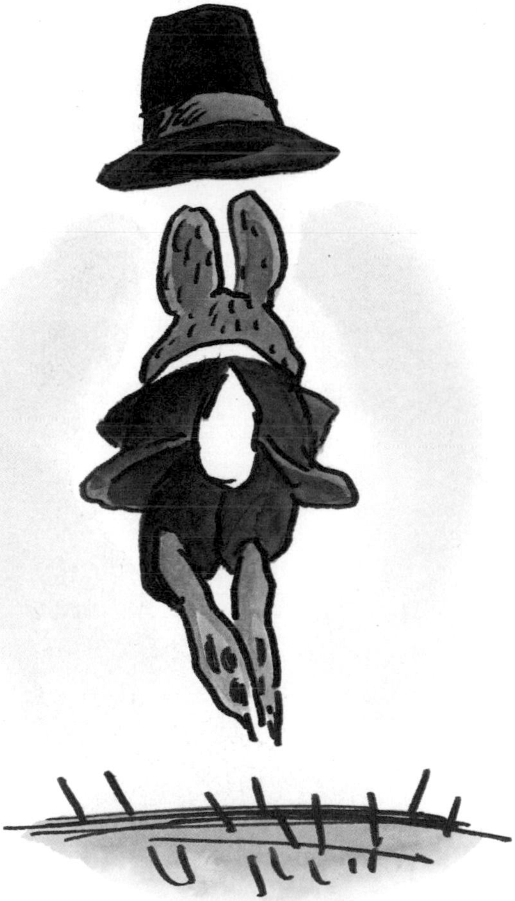

For Dennis – J.M.
For Ella and Kitty – T.R.

This edition published in 1999 by Diamond Books
77–85 Fulham Palace Road,
Hammersmith, London, W6 8JB

First published in Great Britain by Andersen Press Ltd in 1993
First published in Picture Lions in 1994
10 9 8 7 6 5 4 3 2 1
Picture Lions is an imprint of the Children's Division,
part of HarperCollins Publishers Limited,
77–85 Fulham Palace Road, Hammersmith,
London W6 8JB

Printed and bound in Slovenia

CARROT TOPS
and
COTTONTAILS

Written by Jan Mark
Illustrated by Tony Ross

Here is a tale of long ago, in the days when vegetables could talk. None of you has ever heard a vegetable talk.
This is why.

Once upon a time in a green and pleasant valley, there was a hedge. On one side of the hedge lay a field, and in the field lived a colony of peaceable rabbits.

On the other side of the hedge was a garden. In the garden
lived a band of gallant carrots.

At morning and evening the rabbits came out of their burrows and nibbled the grass, and the grass never complained, for the rabbits kept its hair tidy. Under the ground it was busy being grass roots, discussing important matters. Like many clever persons, the grass would never have bothered to get its hair cut – had it not been for the rabbits.

In the mornings the carrots lay in bed with only the plumes on their hats showing, but in the evenings they rose up and basked in the glow of the setting sun. Carrots always look their best at sunset, and these were very vain carrots.

Unlike the grass, the carrots never said anything important. They were too busy admiring themselves and showing off before the other vegetables, the lettuces who were fat and vulgar, the cabbages who had big hearts but no brains, the turnips who were dull and earthy, and the radishes, who were insignificant.

The only things that did not admire the carrots were the rabbits. They were occupied on the far side of the hedge, eating grass, and anyway, they had been taught that it is rude to stare.

The carrots were affronted. They posed, they preened, they twirled the feathers on their hats until even the beetroot turned pale with envy, but the rabbits just went on eating grass.

In the end the carrots could bear it no longer.

"I say!" they shouted. "I say! You there, with the silly ears!"

"Us?" said the friendly rabbits, and they hopped to the hedge where the carrots were jeering in a row.

"Yes, you," said the carrots. "I say, you, *why* do you have such silly cars?"

The rabbits were hurt.

"We do not think our ears are silly," they said. "And they are the only ears we have."

"And silly or not," said the eldest rabbit, "with our ears we can hear our friend the grass."

"Why listen to grass when you could listen to us?" the carrots bawled, but the rabbits turned away and went back to the field. They were very loyal.

The next evening the carrots were there again, flouncing and
flaunting while the other vegetables stood in line to admire them.

"I say!" shouted the carrots. "I say! You there, with the
silly tails!"

"Us?" said the courteous rabbits, and they hurried to the
hedge.

"Yes, you," said the carrots. "I say, you, *why* do you have
such silly tails?"

The rabbits were offended. "We do not think our tails are silly," they said. "And they are the only tails we have."

"And silly or not," said the youngest rabbit, "when one of us turns up his tail and runs, we know that danger is near."

They turned their backs and hopped away. The arrogant carrots saw their bobbing tails and fell about, laughing.

The next evening the carrots were lying in wait for the rabbits,
and when the rabbits came out they began to hoot and hiss.

"I say, I say!" the carrots called. "You there, with the silly
eyes!"

"Us?" said the patient rabbits, and they hastened to the hedge.

"Yes, you!" said the carrots. "I say, you. *Why* do you have
such silly eyes?"

The rabbits were incensed. "We do not think our eyes are silly," they said. "And they are the only eyes we have."

"And silly or not," said the fattest rabbit, "we can see what happens behind us without turning our heads."

They went back to their field without turning their heads to look at the barracking carrots.

"But we can still see you," said the fattest rabbit.

The next evening, when the rabbits came out, the carrots were there in a row by the hedge.

And they all shouted, "I say! I say! You there with the silly teeth!"

"Us?" said the angry rabbits and they hurtled to the hedge.

"Yes, you," cried the carrots. "I say, you, *why* do you have such silly teeth?"

The rabbits were outraged. "We do not think our teeth are silly," they said. "And they are the only teeth we have."

"And silly or not," said the toughest rabbit, "our teeth will bite through anything."

"*Anything?*" sneered the carrots. "Could they bite through a tree? Could they bite through a stone? Could they bite through a brick?"

"No no no," said all the rabbits together. "But they could bite through *you.*"

And then the rabbits thundered under the hedge and fell upon the carrots. The carnage was frightful. Not a carrot remained alive, for though they were rude and fearless, they could not withstand the teeth of the vengeful rabbits.

And when the carrots were slain, the rabbits turned upon the
radishes and the beetroots, the cabbages and lettuces and the
earthy turnips who had gathered round to watch. When night
fell, the garden was laid waste.

And since that time no carrot has been safe in the presence of a hostile rabbit, and all other vegetables fear their terrible teeth. But the rabbits still live in peace and harmony with grass, coming out of their burrows at morning and evening, to trim its hair, while underground the grass roots continue to discuss important matters, and sometimes people ask their opinion.

But no one speaks to vegetables, and vegetables do not speak at all. They dare not.

I once heard of a small farm in Connecticut where on autumn evenings the pumpkins can be heard singing 'God Bless America'.

But that was told to me by a seafaring sheep with one eye.

He may have been lying.

Jan Mark was born in Welwyn, Hertfordshire and grew up in Kent, where she attended the Canterbury College of Art. She taught for six years in a secondary school before becoming a freelance writer in 1974. Since then she has written a number of highly successful novels and short stories for both children and adults and has been awarded many prestigious prizes, including the Carnegie Medal. She now lives in Oxford.

Tony Ross was born in London in 1938. His dream was to work with horses but instead he went to art college in Liverpool. Since then, Tony has worked as an art director at an advertising agency, a graphic designer, a cartoonist, a teacher and

a film maker – as well as illustrating over 250 books! Tony, his wife Zoë and family live in Macclesfield, Cheshire.